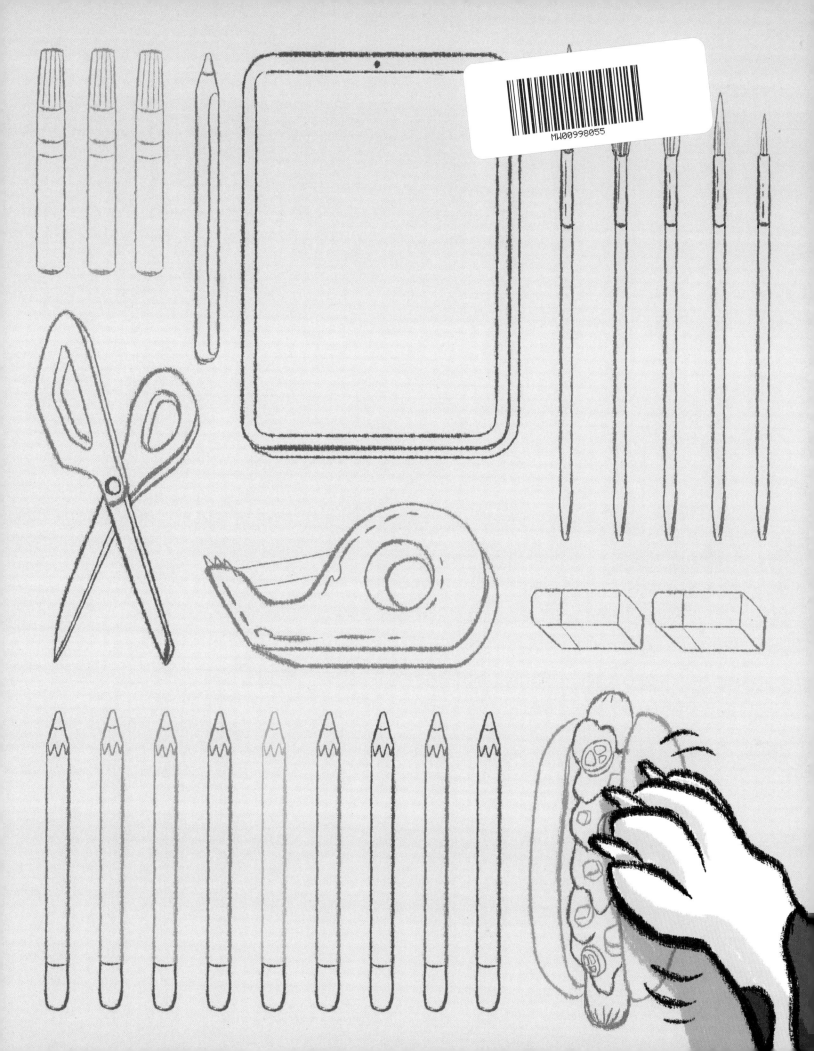

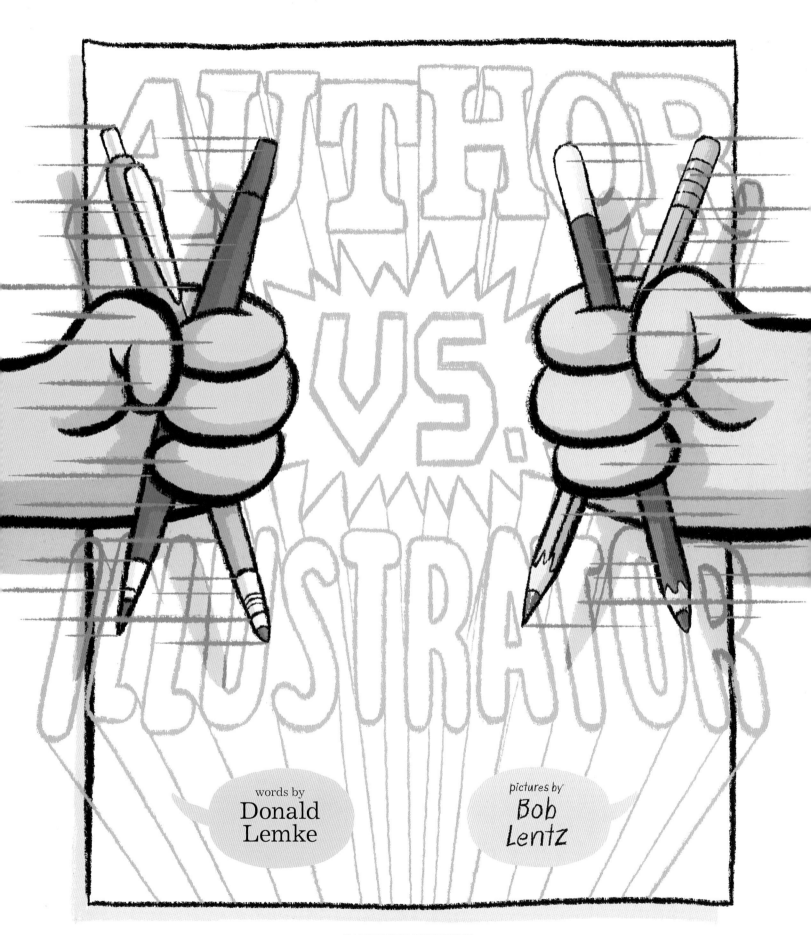

AUTHOR VS. ILLUSTRATOR

words by
Donald Lemke

pictures by
Bob Lentz

CAPSTONE EDITIONS
a capstone imprint

Suddenly, a terrible, completely unexpected snowstorm covered the mountaintop. Nothing but whiteness could be seen. Luckily, Captain Sprinkle, being a far superior superhero, easily navigated through the blinding snow.

With one hand tied behind his back, Captain Sprinkle quickly defeated Sir Swirlsalot, taking him straight to Sprinkletown jail.

To my daughters, who laugh at my jokes (but also think I can draw...)
– Donald

To Mom & Dad, who encouraged me to become an illustrator
– Bob

Published by Capstone Editions, an imprint of Capstone
1710 Roe Crest Drive, North Mankato, Minnesota 56003
capstonepub.com

Library of Congress Cataloging-in-Publication Data is available on the Library of Congress website.
ISBN: 9781684469970 (hardcover)
ISBN: 9781684469987 (ebook PDF)

Summary: At the far reaches of Earth, high upon a mountaintop, a bustling city is under attack by a . . . cute little furball? Wait—what?! That's not right. The author wrote this book about a "ferocious beast," not a cuddly critter. Turns out, the book's illustrator has other plans. Can the author make a successful book with no pictures? Can the illustrator tell a tale without words? Or will this dueling duo get on the same page at last to create the ultimate happy ending?

Printed and bound in China. 5826